The Splish-Splash Puddle Dance!

For my beloved family –P. L.

To my twin sister –C. G.

SIMON SPOTLIGHT
An imprint of Simon & Schuster Children's Publishing Division
1230 Avenue of the Americas, New York, New York 10020
This Simon Spotlight edition December 2023
Text copyright © 2023 by Patricia Lakin
Illustrations copyright © 2023 by Chiara Galletti
SIMON SPOTLIGHT, READY-TO-READ, and colophon are registered
trademarks of Simon & Schuster, Inc.
For information about special discounts for bulk purchases, please contact
Simon & Schuster Special Sales at 1-866-506-1949 or
business@simonandschuster.com.
Manufactured in the United States of America 1023 LAK
10 9 8 7 6 5 4 3 2 1
This book has been cataloged by the Library of Congress.
ISBN 978-1-6659-2010-0 (hc)
ISBN 978-1-6659-2009-4 (pbk)
ISBN 978-1-6659-2011-7 (ebook)

TOW on the GO!
The Splish-Splash Puddle Dance!

Ready-to-Read

Simon Spotlight
New York   London   Toronto   Sydney   New Delhi

Race Car Ro puts up his top.
He waits for the rain to stop.

Rain makes puddles.
"Oh, what fun!"

Ro splish-splashes in each one.

"What a big one!"
Ro starts to grin.

He revs his engine
and dives in.

WHOA! Race Car Ro
sinks down low.
"My, oh my!
How can I go?"

His wheels spin
in mud so thick.

"Tow Truck Mo,
can you come quick?"

But Tow Truck Mo
cannot go . . .

until he plays his radio!

Mambo music
makes Mo go.

He finds Ro
and says,
"Uh-oh!"

"That is no puddle,"
he tells Ro.

"It is a hole.
You cannot go!"

"I will help."
Mo drops his crane.

Mo unhooks
his hook
and chain.

He puts the hook
right under Ro.

With a shake,
Ro says,
"Please, no!"

"Did I hurt you
with the hook?"

"I know," says Mo.
"Use my lasso!"

Mo begins to twirl it round.

Oops!
He missed.
It hits the ground!

"Dancing just might get you free!"

One and two
and swing
and sway.

Soon Ro cheers.
"I'm out! Hooray!
Tow Truck Mo,
thank you!"

"Now let's splash
and mambo, too!"